Beasley's Christmas Party

by C. W. Munger

Based on a story by
Booth Tarkington

A SAMUEL FRENCH ACTING EDITION

SAMUEL FRENCH

FOUNDED 1830

NEW YORK HOLLYWOOD LONDON TORONTO

SAMUELFRENCH.COM

IMPORTANT BILLING AND CREDIT
REQUIREMENTS

All producers of *BEASLEY'S CHRISTMAS PARTY must* give credit to the Author of the Play in all programs distributed in connection with performances of the Play, and in all instances in which the title of the Play appears for the purposes of advertising, publicizing or otherwise exploiting the Play and/or a production. The name of the Author *must* appear on a separate line on which no other name appears, immediately following the title and *must* appear in size of type not less than fifty percent of the size of the title type.

In addition the following credit *must* be given in all programs and publicity information distributed in association with this piece:

Originally produced by KEEN COMPANY
(Carl Forsman, Artistic Director, Wayne Kelton, Executive Director),
Opening Night was December 7, 2008

BEASLEY'S CHRISTMAS PARTY was originally produced off Broadway by Keen Company (Carl Forsman, Artistic Director and Wayne Kelton, Executive Director) at the Clurman Theatre, Theatre Row, New York City. The production was directed by Carl Forsman, with sets by Beowulf Borlett, costumes by Theresa Squire, lights by Josh Bradford, sound by Will Pickens. The dramaturg was Melissa Hardy. The production stage manager was Emily M. Arnold. The assistant stage manager was Joshua Yocom. The production opened on December 8, 2008. The cast was as follows:

TARKINGTON, et al - Tony Ward

BEASLEY, et al - Joseph Collins

ANN APPERTHWAITE, et al - Christa Scott-Reed

CHARACTERS

MAN ONE:
BOOTH

MAN TWO:
BEASLEY
DOWDEN
OLD BOB
SIMEON PECK
EDITOR

WOMAN ONE:
MISS APPERTHWAITE
COUSIN
HAMILTON
MR. MEYERS
GRIST
JOURNAL MAN

NOTE: The play could be performed by one very gifted actor, I think. Or twelve. We used three, in the arrangement above, and it worked out quite nicely.

-*C.W. Munger*

BOOTH. The maple-bordered street was as still as a country Sunday; so quiet that there seemed an echo to my footsteps. It was four o'clock in the morning; clear October moonlight misted through the thinning foliage to the shadowy sidewalk and lay like a transparent silver fog upon the house of my admiration, as I returned from my first night's work on the "Wainwright Morning Despatch."

I'd already marked this house as the finest in Wainwright, our state capitol. On my previous excursions to this metropolis I had been jealous that Spencerville, the county-seat where I lived, had nothing so good. Now, however, I approached its purlieus with a pleasure in it quite unalloyed, for I was at last myself a resident (albeit of only one Day's standing) of Wainwright, and the house – though I had not even an idea who lived there – part of my possessions as a citizen. Moreover, I might enjoy the warmer pride of a next-door-neighbor, for Mrs. Apperthwaite's, where I had taken a room, was just beyond.

It might be difficult to say why I thought it the "finest" house in Wainwright, for a simpler structure would be hard to imagine; it was merely a big, old-fashioned brick house, painted brown and very plain. But it gave back a great deal for your glance, just as some people do.

It looked like a house where there were a grandfather and a grandmother; where holidays were warmly kept; where there were boisterous family reunions to which uncles and aunts, who had been born there, would return from no matter what distances; a house where big turkeys would be on the table often; it looked like a house where they played charades; where there would be long streamers of evergreen and dozens of wreaths of holly at Christmas-time; where there were tearful, happy weddings and great throwings of rice after little brides from the broad front steps: in a word, it was the sort of house to make the hearts of spinsters and bachelors very lonely and wistful – and that is about as near as I can come to my reason for thinking it the finest house in Wainwright.

Suddenly, the spurt of a match took my eye to one of the upper windows, then a steadier glow of orange told me that a lamp was lighted. The window was opened, and a man looked out.

(**BEASLEY** *whistles.*)

I thought that he meant to attract my attention; that something might be wrong; that perhaps some one was needed to go for a doctor. My mistake was immediately evident, however. The man at the window had not seen me.

BEASLEY. *(whistles)* Boy! Boy! Where are you, Simpledoria? Why, THERE you are! He's right there, underneath the window. I'll bring him up. Wait there, Simpledoria! I'll be down in a jiffy and let you in.

BOOTH. Puzzled, I stared at the vacant lawn before me. The clear moonlight revealed it brightly, and it was empty of any living presence.

A light shone in the hallway behind the broad front doors; suddenly one of these was opened.

BEASLEY. Simpledoria, I don't know what to make of you! You might have caught your death of cold, roving out at such an hour. But there, wipe your feet on the mat and come in. You're safe now! Simpledoria is all right – only a little chilled. I'll bring him up to your fire.

BOOTH. I went on my way in a condition of astonishment that engendered, almost, a doubt of my eyes; for if my sight was unimpaired and myself not subject to optical or mental delusion, neither boy nor dog nor bird nor cat, nor any other object of this visible world, had entered that opened door.

It was only a step to Mrs. Apperthwaite's; I let myself in, stole up to my room, went to my window, and stared across the yard at the house next door. But all was dark there now.

I went to bed, and dreamed that I was out at sea in a fog, having embarked on a transparent vessel whose preposterous name, inscribed upon glass life-belts, depending here and there from an invisible rail, was SIMPLEDORIA.

Mrs. Apperthwaite's was a commodious old house, the greater part of it of about the same age, I judged, as its neighbor; but the late Mr. Apperthwaite had caught the building-fever, the tokens of which, in the nature of a cupola and a pair of imposing turrets, were terrifyingly apparent. These romantic misplacements seemed to me not inharmonious with the pleasantly shabby library, where I found editions of Scott, Byron, and Tennyson, complete; some odd volumes of Victor Hugo, of the elder Dumas, of Flaubert, of Gautier, and of Balzac; and of a later decade, there were novels about those delicately tangled emotions experienced by the supreme few, and some thin volumes of rather precious verse.

'Twas amid these romantic scenes that I wondered if the books were a fair mirror of Miss Apperthwaite's mind (I had been told that Mrs. Apperthwaite had a daughter). Mrs. Apperthwaite herself, in her youth, might have sat to an illustrator of IVANHOE or CAMILLE. Reduced, by her husband's insolvency (coincident with his demise) to "keeping boarders," she did it gracefully, as I learned at lunch that afternoon.

I decided the instant my eye fell upon the lady who sat opposite me that she was Miss Apperthwaite; she "went so," as they say, with her mother. Mrs. Apperthwaite was the kind of woman whom you would expect to have a beautiful daughter, and Miss Apperthwaite more than fulfilled her mother's promise.

Only one other of my own sex was present at the lunchtable, a Mr. Dowden, an elderly lawyer and politician of whom I had heard.

It might have been better mannered for me to address myself to Mr. Dowden, than to open a conversation with Miss Apperthwaite; but I didn't stop to think of that.

"You have a splendid old house next door to you here, Miss Apperthwaite, it's a privilege to find it in view from my window. May I ask who lives there?"

MISS APPERTHWAITE. *(slight pause)* "A Mr. Beasley,"

BOOTH. "Not the Honorable David Beasley!"

MISS APPERTHWAITE. "Yes. Do you know him?"

BOOTH. "Not in person; but I've written a good deal about him. I was with the 'Spencerville Journal' until a few days ago, and even in the country we know who's who in politics over the state. Beasley's the man that went to Congress and never made a speech – never made even a motion to adjourn – but got everything his district wanted. There's talk of him now for Governor."

MISS APPERTHWAITE. "Indeed?"

BOOTH. "And so it's the Honorable David Beasley who lives in that splendid place. How curious that is!"

MISS APPERTHWAITE. "Why?"

BOOTH. "It seems too big for one man, and I've always had the impression Mr. Beasley was a bachelor."

MISS APPERTHWAITE. "Yes, he is."

BOOTH. "But of course he doesn't live there all alone, probably he has – "

MISS APPERTHWAITE. "No. There's no one else – except a colored servant."

BOOTH. "What a crime! If there ever was a house meant for a large family, that one is. Can't you almost hear it crying out for heaps and heaps of romping children? I should think – "

DOWDEN. *(coughs)* "Can you tell me, what the farmers were getting for their wheat when you left Spencerville?"

BOOTH. "Ninety-four cents."

Too late, I remembered that the new-comer in a community should guard his tongue among the natives until he has unraveled the skein of their relationships.

I could only conclude that some unpleasantness had arisen between Dowden and Beasley, probably of political origin, since they were both in politics, and of personal (and consequently bitter) development.

After lunch, not having to report at "the Despatch" immediately, I took unto myself the solace of a stroll about Mrs. Apperthwaite's capacious yard. In the rear I found an old-fashioned rose-garden – the bushes long since bloomless and now brown with autumn – and I paced its gravelled paths up and down, at the same time favoring Mr. Beasley's house with a covert study that would have done credit to a porch-climber, for the sting of my blunder at the table was neutralized under the itch of a curiosity far from satisfied concerning the interesting premises next door. The gentleman at the window could have been no other than the Honorable David Beasley himself. He came not in eyeshot now, neither he nor any other; there was no sign of life about the place. That portion of his yard which lay behind the house was not within my vision, his property being here separated from Mrs. Apperthwaite's by a board fence; there was no sound from the other side of this partition, save that caused by the quiet movement of rusty leaves in the breeze.

Suddenly Miss Apperthwaite appeared bearing a saucer of milk, followed hastily by a very white, fat cat, with a pink ribbon round its neck.

MISS APPERTHWAITE. "I'm almost at the age, you see."

BOOTH. "What age?"

MISS APPERTHWAITE. "When we take to cats. 'Spinsterhood' we like to call it. 'Single-blessedness!'"

BOOTH. "That is your kind heart. You decline to make one of us happy to the despair of all the rest."

(She laughs, halfheartedly.)

MISS APPERTHWAITE. "You seemed interested in the old place next door."

BOOTH. "Oh, I understand my blunder. I wish I'd known the subject was embarrassing or unpleasant to Mr. Dowden."

MISS APPERTHWAITE. "What made you think that?"

BOOTH. "Surely, you saw how pointedly he cut me off."

MISS APPERTHWAITE. "Yes, he rather did. At least, I see how you got that impression. It is an interesting old place."

BOOTH. "And Mr. Beasley himself – "

MISS APPERTHWAITE. "HE isn't interesting. That's his trouble!"

BOOTH. "You mean his trouble not to – "

MISS APPERTHWAITE. "I mean he's a man of no imagination."

BOOTH. "No imagination!"

MISS APPERTHWAITE. "None in the world! Not one ounce of imagination! Not one grain!"

BOOTH. "Then who, or what – is Simpledoria?"

MISS APPERTHWAITE. "Simple – what?"

BOOTH. "Doria."

MISS APPERTHWAITE. "Simpledoria? What in the world is that?"

BOOTH. "You never heard of it before?"

MISS APPERTHWAITE. "Never."

BOOTH. "You've lived next door to Mr. Beasley a long time, haven't you?"

MISS APPERTHWAITE. "All my life."

BOOTH. "And I suppose you must know him pretty well."

MISS APPERTHWAITE. *(smiling)* "What next?"

BOOTH. "You said he lives there all alone."

MISS APPERTHWAITE. "Except for Old Bob, his servant."

BOOTH. "Can you tell me – Has he ever been thought – well, 'peculiar'?"

MISS APPERTHWAITE. "Never! Never anything so exciting! Merely deadly and hopelessly commonplace. What was it about – what was that name? – 'Simpledoria'?"

BOOTH. "I will tell you."

And I related in detail the singular performance of which I had been a witness in the late moonlight before that morning's dawn.

"One explanation might be just barely possible; if it is, it is the most remarkable case of somnambulism on record. Did you ever hear of Mr. Beasley's walking in his – "

BEASLEY. "HERE we come!

MISS APPERTHWAITE. "Shhh!"

BEASLEY. "Me and big Bill Hammersley. I want to show Bill I can jump ANYWAYS three times as far as he can! Come on, Bill."

BOOTH. *(whispers:)* "Is that Mr. Beasley?"

MISS APPERTHWAITE. *(nods)*

BOOTH. *(whispers:)* "Could he have heard me?"

MISS APPERTHWAITE. *(whispers:)* "No, He's just come out of the house. Who under heaven is Bill Hammersley?"

BEASLEY. "Of course, Bill, if you're afraid I'll beat you TOO badly, you've still got time to back out. I did understand you to kind of hint that you were considerable of a jumper, but if – What? What'd you say, Bill?" *(silence)* "Oh, all right, You say you're in this to win, do you? Well, so'm I, Bill Hammersley; so'm I. Who'll go first? Me? All right – from the edge of the walk here. Now then! One – two – three! HA!" *(jump; groan)* "Ugh! Don't you laugh, Bill Hammersley! I haven't jumped as much as I OUGHT to, these last twenty years; I reckon I've kind of lost the hang of it. Now, it's your turn, Bill. What say?" *(silence)* Yes, I'll make Simpledoria get out of the way. Come here, Simpledoria. Now, Bill, put your heels together on the edge of the walk. That's right. All ready? Now then! One for the money – two for the show – three to make ready – and four for to GO! By jingo, Bill Hammersley, you've beat me! That WAS a jump! It's eleven feet if it's an inch. What say?" *(silence)* You say you can do even better than that? Now, Bill, don't brag. Oh! you say you've often jumped farther? Oh! you say that was up in Scotland, where you had a spring-board? All right; What? You say you want to try it again off the side porch? Very well then, off we go!"

MISS APPERTHWAITE. "There was no one THERE! He was all by himself! It was just the same as what you saw last night!"

BOOTH. "Evidently."

MISS APPERTHWAITE. "Did it sound to you – did it sound to you like a person who'd lost his MIND?"

BOOTH. "I don't know. I don't know at all what to make of it."

MISS APPERTHWAITE. "He couldn't have been – intoxicated?!"

BOOTH. "No. I'm sure it wasn't that."

MISS APPERTHWAITE. "Then I don't know what to make of it, either. All that wild talk about 'Bill Hammersley' and 'Simpledoria' and spring-boards in Scotland!"

BOOTH. "And an eleven-foot jump."

MISS APPERTHWAITE. "Why, there's no more a 'Bill Hammersley,' than there is a 'Simpledoria'!"

BOOTH. "So it appears."

MISS APPERTHWAITE. "He's lived there all alone, in that big house, so long, just sitting there evening after evening all by himself, never going out, never reading anything, not even thinking; but just sitting and sitting and sitting and SITTING – Well, there's no use bothering one's own head about it."

BOOTH. "I'm glad to have a fellow-witness; It's so eerie I might have concluded there was something the matter with ME."

MISS APPERTHWAITE. "You're going to work? I'm very glad I don't have to go to mine."

BOOTH. "Yours?"

MISS APPERTHWAITE. "I teach algebra and plain geometry at the High School. Thank Heaven, it's Saturday! I'm reading Les Miserables for the seventh time, and I'm going to have a real ORGY over Gervaise and the barricade this afternoon!"

BOOTH. I don't know why it should have astonished me to learn that Miss Apperthwaite was a teacher of mathematics except that (to my inexperienced eye) she didn't look it. She looked more like ANNA KARENINA!

As I began to know some of my co-laborers on the "Despatch," and to pick up acquaintances here and there about town, I sometimes made Mr. Beasley the subject of inquiry. Mr. Meyers at the Five and Dime expounded readily:

MR. MEYERS. "Oh yes, I know Dave BEASLEY! He is the quiet type. The first and readiest prey for every fraud and swindler that comes to Wainwright, too kind by half. But in spite of this he has a large practice, and he's one of the most successful lawyers in the state! Pretty remarkable especially since he almost never says more than five words in a row."

BOOTH. One story told of him (or, as folks were more apt to put it, "on" him) was repeated so often that I saw it had become one of the town's traditions. My editor at the paper explained:

EDITOR. One bitter evening in February, Dave was approached in the street by a shivering old reprobate. A delinquent type. So notorious for his schemes that he had worn out the patience of all the charity organizations. He asked Beasley for a dime. Beasley had no ready money, but gave the man his overcoat, went home shivering himself, and spent six weeks in bed with a bad case of pneumonia as the direct result. Now the old drunk sold the overcoat, and invested the proceeds in a five-day spree, with a couple of bricks featured in a spectacular finale. One he sent through a jeweler's show-window in an attempt to intimidate some imaginary pursuers, the other he projected at an ACTUAL policeman. The victim of Beasley's charity and the officer both spent the night up in the hospital.

BOOTH. It was due in part to recollections like this and others of a similar character that people laughed when they said,

EDITOR. "Oh yes, I know Dave BEASLEY!"

BOOTH. Altogether, I should say, Beasley was about the most popular man in Wainwright. I could discover nowhere anything, however, to shed the faintest light upon the mystery of Bill Hammersley and Simpledoria. The next afternoon I went to call upon the widow of a second-cousin of mine; she lived in a cottage not far from Mrs. Apperthwaite's, upon the same street.

We sat on her pleasant veranda and exchanged news of mutual relatives. I had told her how I liked my work and what I thought of Wainwright, when she interrupted me to smile and nod a cordial greeting to two gentlemen driving by in a carriage. And if ever two men were obviously and incontestably on the best of terms with each other, THESE two were. They were David Beasley and Mr. Dowden.

COUSIN. "I do wish dear David Beasley would get a new trap of some kind; that old carriage of his is a disgrace! I suppose you haven't met him yet? Living at Mrs. Apperthwaite's, you wouldn't be apt to."

BOOTH. "But what is he doing with Mr. Dowden?"

COUSIN. "Taking him for a drive, I suppose."

BOOTH. "No. I mean – how do they happen to be together?"

COUSIN. "Why shouldn't they be? They're old friends – "

BOOTH. "But when I once began to speak of Mr. Beasley, Mr. Dowden abruptly changed the subject!'

COUSIN. "I see. That's simple enough. George Dowden didn't want you to talk of Beasley THERE. I suppose it may have been a little embarrassing for everybody – especially if Ann Apperthwaite heard you."

BOOTH. "Miss Apperthwaite? Yes; I was speaking directly to her. Why SHOULDN'T she have heard me? She talked of him herself – and at some length, too."

COUSIN. "She DID! Well, of all!"

BOOTH. "Is it so surprising?"

COUSIN. "Ann Apperthwaite thinks about him still! I've
always suspected it. She thought you were new to the
place and didn't know anything about it all, or
anybody to mention it to. That's it!"

BOOTH. "I'm still new to the place, and I still don't know
anything about it."

COUSIN. "They used to be engaged."

BOOTH. "Oh. Ohhhhh!"

COUSIN. "I'm glad she DOES think of him, it serves her
right. I only hope HE won't find it out, because he's
a poor, faithful creature; he'd jump at the chance to
take her back – and she doesn't deserve him."

BOOTH. "How long has it been since they were engaged?"

COUSIN. "Oh, a good while – five or six years, I think –
maybe more; time skips along. Ann Apperthwaite's
no chicken, you know. They got engaged just after
she came home from college, and of all the idiotically
romantic girls – "

BOOTH. "But she's a teacher of mathematics."

COUSIN. "Yes. I always thought that explained it: the
romance is a reaction from the algebra. I never knew
a person connected with mathematics or astronomy or
statistics, or any of those exact things, who didn't have
a crazy streak in 'em SOMEwhere. They've got to blow
off steam and be foolish to make up for putting in so
much of their time at hard sense. But don't you think
that I dislike Ann Apperthwaite. She's always been one
of my best friends; that's why I feel at liberty to abuse
her – and I always will abuse her when I think how she
treated poor David Beasley."

BOOTH. "How did she treat him?"

COUSIN. "Threw him over out of a clear sky one night,
that's all. Just sent him home and broke his heart; that
is, it would have been broken if he'd had any kind of
disposition except the one the Lord blessed him with

– just all optimism and cheerfulness and make-the-best-of-it-ness! He's never cared for anybody else, and I guess he never will."

BOOTH. "What did she do it for?"

COUSIN. "NOTHING! Nothing in the wide WORLD!"

BOOTH. "But there must have been – "

COUSIN. "Listen to me, and tell me if you ever heard anything queerer in your life. They'd been engaged – Heaven knows how long – over two years; probably nearer three – and always she kept putting it off; wouldn't begin to get ready, wouldn't set a day for the wedding. Then Mr. Apperthwaite died, and left her and her mother stranded high and dry with nothing to live on. David had everything in the world to give her – and STILL she wouldn't! And then, one day, she came up here and told me she'd broken it off. Said she couldn't stand it to be engaged to David Beasley another minute!"

BOOTH. "But why?"

COUSIN. "Because she said he was a man of no imagination!"

BOOTH. "She still says so!'

COUSIN. "Then it's time she got a little imagination herself! David Beasley's the quietest man God has made, but everybody knows what he IS! There are some rare people in this world that aren't all TALK; there are some still rarer ones that scarcely ever talk at all – and David Beasley's one of them. I don't know whether it's because he can't talk, or if he can and hates to; I only know he doesn't. And I'm glad of it, and thank the Lord he's put a few like that into this talky world! David Beasley's does better than talk. He THINKS! The trouble with Ann Apperthwaite was that she was too young to see it. She was so full of novels and poetry and dreaminess and highfalutin' nonsense she couldn't see ANYTHING as it really was. She just couldn't bear to have a fiancé who hadn't any chance of turning out to be the crown-prince of Kenosha in disguise! Oh, you should have heard her talk about it! –

MISS APPERTHWAITE. 'I couldn't bear it another day, I couldn't STAND it! In all the time I've known him I don't believe he's ever asked me a single question – except when he asked if I'd marry him. He never says ANYTHING – never speaks at ALL!

COUSIN. 'You don't know a blessing when you see it.'

MISS APPERTHWAITE. 'Blessing! There's nothing IN the man! He has no DEPTHS! He hasn't any more imagination than the chair he sits and sits and sits in! Half the time he answers what I say to him by nodding with that foolish, contented smile of his. I'd have gone MAD if it had lasted any longer!'

COUSIN. Do you think married life consists very largely of conversations between husband and wife?

MISS APPERTHWAITE. "Even married life ought to have some POETRY in it. 'Some romance, some soul! And he just comes and sits, and sits and sits and sits and sits! And I can't bear it any longer, and I've told him so.'"

BOOTH. "Poor Mr. Beasley."

COUSIN. "Poor Ann Apperthwaite! I'd like to know if there's anything NICER than just to sit and sit and sit and sit with as lovely a man as that – a man who understands things, and thinks and listens and smiles – instead of everlastingly talking!"

BOOTH. "As it happens, I've heard Mr. Beasley talk."

COUSIN. "Why, of course he talks, when there's any real use in it. And he talks to children; he's THAT kind of man."

BOOTH. "I meant a particular instance," and for the second time I related the mystery of Simpledoria and Bill Hammersley, hoping she might have some clue.

COUSIN. "I never heard of any Simplewhoosit, or Bill Whatshisname. Maybe the dear fellow has gone mad. Would serve Ann Apperthwaite right! Poor thing."

BOOTH. Once more baffled, I returned to Mrs.

Apperthwaite's – and within the hour came into full possession of the very heart of that dark and subtle mystery which overhung the house next door and so perplexed my soul.

Finding that I had still some leisure before me, I got a book from the library and repaired to the bench in the garden. But I did not read; I had but opened the book when I heard:

OLD BOB. "Ah met mah sistuh in a-mawnin',

She 'uz a-waggin' up de hill SO slow!

'Sistuh, you mus' git a rastle in doo time,

B'fo de hevumly do's cloze – iz!'"

"Lay still, honey. Des keep on a-nappin' an' a-breavin' de f'esh air. Dass wha's go' mek you good an' well agin."

HAMILTON. *(offstagfe)* "I – want – I – want – Bill – Hammersley!"

BOOTH. The shabby carriage which had passed my cousin's house was drawing up to the curb near Beasley's gate.

OLD BOB. "Hi dar! Look at dat! Hain' Bill a comin' yonnah des edzacly on de dot an' to de vey spot an' instink when you 'quiah fo' 'im, honey? Dar come Mist' Dave, right on de minute, an' you kin bet yo' las hunnud dollahs he got dat Bill Hammersley wif 'im! Come along, honey-chile! Ah's go' to pull you 'roun in de side yod fo' to meet 'em."

BOOTH. Mr. Dowden jumped out of the carriage with a wave to the driver (Beasley himself) and advanced to meet me.

DOWDEN. "Some day I want to take you over next door. You ought to know Beasley, especially as I hear you're doing some political reporting. Dave Beasley's going to be the next governor of this state, you know."

BOOTH. "From all I hear, you ought to know who'll get it."

DOWDEN. *(chuckles)* "I expect you thought I shifted the subject pretty briskly the other day? I meant to tell you about that, but the opportunity didn't occur. You see –"

BOOTH. "I understand, I've heard the story. You thought it might be embarrassing to Miss Apperthwaite."

DOWDEN. "I expect I was pretty clumsy about it. It's a mighty strange case. Here they keep on living next door to each other, year after year, each going on alone when they might just as well… They bow when they happen to meet, but they haven't exchanged a word since the night she sent him away, long ago. Well, sir, Dave's got something at home to keep him busy enough, these days, I expect!"

BOOTH. "Do you mind telling me? Is its name 'Simpledoria'?"

DOWDEN. "Lord, no! What on earth made you think that?"

BOOTH. I told him. It was my third success with this narrative.

DOWDEN. "So I expect you must have decided that David Beasley has gone just plain, plum insane."

BOOTH. "Well…

DOWDEN. "Now, I'll tell you all there is TO it. You see, Dave grew up with a cousin of his named Hamilton Swift; they were boys together; went to the same school, and then to college. I don't believe there was ever a high word spoken between them. Nobody in this life ever got a quarrel out of Dave Beasley, and Hamilton Swift was a mighty good sort of a fellow, too. He went East to live, after they got out of college, yet they always managed to get together once a year, generally about Christmas-time; you couldn't pass them on the street without hearing their laughter ringing out louder than the sleigh-bells, maybe over some old joke between them, or some fool thing they did, perhaps, when they were boys. But finally Hamilton Swift's business took him over to the other side of the water to live; and he married an English girl, an orphan without any kin. That was about ten years ago. Well, sir, this last summer he and his wife were taking a trip down in Switzerland, and they were both drowned – tipped over out of a rowboat in Lake Lucerne – and word came that Hamilton Swift's will appointed Dave guardian of the one child they had, a little boy – Hamilton Swift,

Junior's his name. He was sent across the ocean in charge of a doctor, and Dave went on to New York to meet him. He brought him home here the very day before you passed the house and saw poor Dave getting up at four in the morning to let that ghost in. And a mighty funny ghost Simpledoria is!"

BOOTH. "I begin to understand, and to feel pretty silly, too."

DOWDEN. "Not at all, that little chap's inventions would mystify anybody. You see, this poor little cuss has a complication of infirmities that have kept him on his back most of his life, never knowing other children, never playing, or anything; He was born sick, as I understand it – his bones and nerves and insides are all wrong.

Of course, most children have make-believe friends and companions, but this lonely little feller's got HIS people worked out in his mind and materialized beyond any I ever heard of. Dave got well acquainted with 'em on the train on the way home, and they certainly are giving him a lively time. Ho, ho! Getting him up at four in the morning – "

"Simpledoria – now where do you suppose he got that name? – well, Simpledoria is supposed to be Hamilton Swift, Junior's St. Bernard dog. Beasley had to BATHE him the other day, he told me! And Bill Hammersley is supposed to be a boy of Hamilton Swift, Junior's own age, but very big and strong; he has rosy cheeks, and he can do more in athletics than a whole college track-team. That's the reason he out-jumped Dave so far, you see."

BOOTH. Miss Apperthwaite was at home the following Saturday. I found her in the library with Les Miserables on her knee when I came down from my room a little before lunch-time; and she looked up and gave me a smile that made me feel sorry for any one she had ceased to smile upon.

"I wanted to tell you, I've found out that I'm an awful fool."

MISS APPERTHWAITE. "But that's something. At least the beginning of wisdom."

BOOTH. "I mean about Mr. Beasley – the mystery I was absurd enough to find in 'Simpledoria.' I want to tell you – "

MISS APPERTHWAITE. "Oh, I know, I've heard all about it. Mr. Beasley's been appointed trustee or something for poor Hamilton Swift's son, a little invalid boy who invents all sorts of characters. Old Bob told our cook about Bill Hammersley and Simpledoria. So, you see, I understand."

BOOTH. "I'm glad you do."

MISS APPERTHWAITE. "And I'm glad there's SOMEbody in that house, at last, with a little imagination!"

BOOTH. "From everything I have heard, it would be difficult to say which has more – Mr. Beasley or the child."

MISS APPERTHWAITE. *(She is tearing up.)* "I'm just finishing the death of Jean Valjean, you know, in Les Miserables. I'm always afraid I'll cry over that. I try not to, because it makes my eyes red." *(She's off.)*

BOOTH. That afternoon, when I reached the "Despatch" office, I was summoned to see my editor.

EDITOR. "Now I need you to go over to David Beasley's office and see if you can't get anything out of him. He's running for Governor, and even though he's well liked and he's apt to get elected without making a single speech, well, we ought to try to get him to talk about something! You're new around here, so maybe you can get him to open up. Good luck! Personally, I've never heard him say three sentences in a row.

BOOTH. He was a true prophet.

I found the Honourable David Beasley looking over some documents in his office. I began at once to put my interrogations to him.

I asked after the cigarette ban.

BEASLEY. I'm fer it.

BOOTH. And the County Option Law.

BEASLEY. Fer that too.

BOOTH. I asked after his position on the banning of Benzoate of soda, recently introduced into the state legislature.

BOOTH. Not sure.

BOOTH. In a desperate attempt to get him talking, I asked if he had an opinion on the banning of the hammer throw at statewide track and field meets, to which he replied,

BEASLEY. "Well – about that – "

BOOTH. "Yes?"

BEASLEY. "About that –

BOOTH. "Yes?"

BEASLEY. "I suppose – "

BOOTH. "Yes, Mr. Beasley?"

BEASLEY. "Well, sir – Hadn't you better see some one else about THAT?"

My note-book remained almost noteless.

I finally asked him what he made of the current situation in Europe, an invitation so expansive I believed no politician could fail to answer it. At length he answered:

BEASLEY. Curious.

(Their eyes meet. They laugh.)

BOOTH. I never met anybody who looked so pleasantly communicative and managed to say so little. I guessed that this faculty was not without its value in his political career, disastrous as it had proved to his private happiness.

Two or three days after that, as I started down-town from Mrs. Apperthwaite's, Beasley came out of his gate, bound in the same direction.

BEASLEY. "WELL! Up in THIS neighborhood!" *(They shake.)*

BOOTH. I'm a neighbor, boarding at Mrs. Apperthwaite's.

BEASLEY. You don't say.

BOOTH. And for the rest of the walk he fell silent. But he listened visibly to my own talk, and laughed at everything that I meant for funny.

He seemed to be WITH you every instant; I never knew anybody who gave one a greater responsiveness.

It happened that I thus met him, as we were both starting down-town, and walked on with him several days in succession; in a word, it became a habit.

Then, one afternoon:

BEASLEY. Maybe tomorrow before we leave you'll drop over for a cigar before we start?

BOOTH. As this qualified as an eloquent and rambling invitation from the Honorable David Beasley, I thought it only polite to say:

"Glad to."

BEASLEY. "Good."

BOOTH. And he asked me if I wouldn't come again the next day. So this became a habit, too.

A fortnight elapsed before I met Hamilton Swift, Junior. We had just finished our cigars in Beasley's airy, old-fashioned "sitting-room". We were rising to go, when there came the faint creaking of small wheels from the hall.

BEASLEY. "I've got a little chap here."

BOOTH. Old Bob appeared in the doorway pulling a little wagon, and in it sat Hamilton Swift, Junior.

BOOTH. My first impression of him was that he was all eyes: I couldn't look at anything else for a time, and was hardly conscious of the rest of that under-sized wisp of a body.

BEASLEY. "HOO-ray!"

HAMILTON. "Br-r-ra-vo!"

BEASLEY. "Who's with us to-day?"

HAMILTON. "I'm MISTER Swift, MIS-TER Swift, if you please, Cousin David Beasley."

BEASLEY. *(bows)* "There is a gentleman here who'd like to meet you. This is my newest acquaintance, he's a journalist over at the paper downtown, a nice fellow with a keen sense of humor. Sir, this is Mister swift."

HAMILTON. "I am pleased to meet you, sir. "

BOOTH. "The pleasure is mine, Mr. Swift."

HAMILTON. "And besides me, there's Bill Hammersley and Mr. Corley Linbridge."

(a brief pause)

BOOTH. "I have heard from Mr. Dowden of Bill Hammersley, though until now I am a stranger to the fame of Mr. Corley Linbridge. I would be delighted to be introduced to them both."

BEASLEY. "Mister Swift's acquaintance Mr. William Hammersley, *(They shake.)* Master Hammersly, I am pleased to introduce you to the newest reporter over at the Despatch.

BOOTH. "Hello, William."

HAMILTON. "And I am sure as a man of journalistic interest you will have heard of the distinguished Mr. Corley Linbridge?" *(They shake.)*

BOOTH. "An honor to meet you, Mr. Linbridge."

HAMILTON. "And Simpledoria! You'll enjoy Simpledoria."

BEASLEY. St. Bernard, don't you know.

BOOTH. "Hello, Simpledoria. Can he shake hands? Some dogs can."

HAMILTON. "Watch him! Simpledoria, shake hands!"

BOOTH. *(shakes the dog's paw)* In this wise was my initiation into the beautiful old house and the cordiality of its inmates completed; and I became a familiar of David Beasley and his ward.

The order of the day with him always began with the...

BEASLEY. "HOO-ray!"

HAMILTON. "BR-R-RA-vo!"

BOOTH. Of greeting; after which we were to inquire...

BEASLEY. "Who's with us to-day?"

BOOTH. Whereupon he would make known the character in which he elected to be received for the occasion. If he announced himself as...

HAMILTON. "Mister Swift,"

BOOTH. Everything was to be very grown-up and decorous indeed. Formalities and distances were observed; and Mr. Corley Linbridge (an elderly personage of great dignity and distinction as a mountain-climber, it turned out) was much oftener included in the conversation than Bill Hammersley. If, however, he declared himself to be...

HAMILTON. "Hamilton Swift, Junior,"

BOOTH. Which was his happiest mood, Bill Hammersley and Simpledoria were in the ascendant, and there were games and contests. On one of the Hamilton Swift, Jr. days Beasley and I were narrowly defeated by Dowden and Bill Hammersley in a closely contested three-legged race.

HAMILTON. "Bill Hammersley wins again!"

BOOTH. Old Bob was also amused.

OLD BOB. OH, that was close.

BOOTH. He had a third title for himself:

HAMILTON. "Just little Hamilton";

BOOTH. But this was only when the creaky voice could hardly chirp at all and the weazened face was drawn to one side with suffering. When he told us he was...

HAMILTON. "Just little Hamilton"

BOOTH. We were all very quiet.

Once his Invisibles all went away on a visit: Hamilton Swift, Junior, had become interested in bears.

HAMILTON. "Cousin David, Cousin David, come quick, there's a Grizzly and a Brown in the parlor!"

BOOTH. But after ten days the bears were dismissed abruptly: Bill Hammersley and Mr. Corley Linbridge and Simpledoria came trooping back, and with them they brought that wonderful family, the Hunchbergs.

Beasley had just opened the front door when Hamilton Swift, Junior announced:

HAMILTON. "Cousin David Beasley! The Hunchbergs are here!"

BEASLEY. "The Hunchbergs?"

BOOTH. Old Bob had already met them.

OLD BOB. "Yassir, I jez bin introduce my own self. They's quite a family."

HAMILTON. "They like Bob, Don't you, Mr. Hunchberg? Yes, he says they do extremely!"

OLD BOB. "I's glad."

HAMILTON. "And I'm sure, that all the family will admire Cousin David. Yes, Mr. Hunchberg says, he thinks they will."

BEASLEY. "Well Mister Hunchberg, of course you are welcome in my home! I'd like to offer you a cigar."

BOOTH. I met the Hunchberg family, myself, the day after their arrival.

BEASLEY. This is Mr. Hunchberg, you will be pleased to make his acquaintance as he is a very generous, kindly, upstanding, patriarch.

BOOTH. Hello Sir.

BEASLEY. And this is Mrs. Hunchberg, who I hope I will not embarrass too much if I tell you she is a very lively sort.

BOOTH. Nice to meet you, ma'am.

BEASLEY. And these here are the Hunchberg boys – this here is Mr. Tom, this is Mr. Noble, and this is Mr. Grandee

HAMILTON. Grandee is just a year older than me!

BEASLEY. And something of a troublemaker too, aren't you Grandee!

HAMILTON. He is, he is!

BOOTH. I'll be sure to watch myself. Hello, boys.

BEASLEY. And these are Mrs. Hunchberg's beautiful daughters. This is Miss Queen.

BOOTH. Hello.

BEASLEY. Miss Marble.

BOOTH. Charmed.

BEASLEY. And Miss Molanna. Don't pull her pigtails, Grandee!

HAMILTON. She's the youngest!

BOOTH. It's very nice to meet you. What a large family!

HAMILTON. Don't forget –

BEASLEY. Indeed, I would be remiss if I did not introduce you to Colonel Hunchberg, whose bravery and heartiness we all admire.

BOOTH. It's an honor, sir.

BEASLEY. And this is Aunt Cooley. *(shouting)* SAY HELLO TO OUR NEIGHBOR, AUNT COOLEY!

HAMILTON. She's a bit deaf.

BOOTH. I see. IT'S VERY NICE TO MAKE YOUR ACQUAINTANCE.

BEASLEY. And we are fortunate that Mr. Corley Linbridge is calling today as well! It's quite a housefull.

BOOTH. Indeed. Hello sir.

HAMILTON. Mr. Linbridge was telling us about his trip to Kilimanjaro!

BEASLEY. The mountain in Africa. *(to Aunt Cooley:)* KILIMANJARO! Mr. Tom is interested in becoming an adventurer as well.

HAMILTON. Or a sea captain!

BEASLEY. Or a spelunker!

BOOTH. I see. Has the Colonel ever been to Africa?

HAMILTON. Of course he has!

BEASLEY. The Colonel spent many years in the dark continent,

HAMILTON. Hunting Lions!

BEASLEY. Indeed, he once had to fight off an angry lion with just a fireplace poker and a frying pan!

HAMILTON. How extraordinary!

BOOTH. Impressive.

HAMILTON. The Hunchbergs say it's time for charades!

BEASLEY. Very good. WOULD YOU LIKE TO PLAY CHARADES, AUNT COOLEY?

BOOTH. The Hunchbergs had lately moved to Wainwright from Constantinople, I learned; they had decided not to live in town, however, having purchased a fine farm out in the country, and, on account of the distance, were able to call at Beasley's only about eight times a day, and seldom more than twice in the evening.

On one occasion when Mr. Hunchberg and I happened to be calling, a very serious incident occurred.

HAMILTON. Cousin David! Cousin David! Did you see Simpledoria come in?

BEASLEY. Why no, I was just talking with Mr. Hunchberg about summering in Romania.

HAMILTON. Simpledoria came in and he didn't lick my hand. Instead he crawled right under that table!

BEASLEY. I see.

HAMILTON. What do you suppose could be the matter with him?

BEASLEY. I couldn't say. What's that Mr. Hunchberg? Oh, I see.

HAMILTON. What's happened?

BEASLEY. I'm sorry to say, Mr. Hunchberg informs me that he saw Simpledoria chasing a small cat around the yard earlier.

HAMILTON. Oh no.

BOOTH. I regret to say, I saw the same thing.

HAMILTON. Oh no! Not the cat that belongs to that pretty lady next door?

BOOTH. No, another cat.

HAMILTON. Naughty Simpledoria!

BEASLEY. Oh, yes, Mr. Hunchberg, I agree.

HAMILTON. Bad doggie! What's that?

BEASLEY. Mr. Hunchberg suggests that Simpledoria is hiding under the table because he knows that he has behaved wickedly. Perhaps we should forgive him and trust that he will not repeat this vile behavior. What do you think, Hamilton?

HAMILTON. All right. Come on out, Simpledoria. I forgive you!

BEASLEY. Yes Simpledoria, come on out now! Here he is!

HAMILTON. You forgive him, don't you, Cousin David?

BEASLEY. I do.

HAMILTON. And, you forgive him, don't you, Mr. Hunchberg?

BEASLEY. He does.

HAMILTON. And you do, don't you sir?

BOOTH. I do. (**BEASLEY** *pets Simledoria.*) I forgive you, Simpledora.

BEASLEY. Sit up! Good boy.

BOOTH. Autumn trailed the last leaves behind her flying brown robes one night; we woke to a skurry of snow next morning; and it was winter. Down-town, along the sidewalks, the merchants set lines of poles, covered them with evergreen, and ran streamers of green overhead to encourage the festal shopping. Salvation Army Santa Clauses stamped their feet and rang bells on the corners, and pink-faced children fixed their noses immovably to display-windows. For them, the season of seasons, the time of times, was at hand.

To a certain new reporter on the "Despatch" the stir and gayety of the streets meant little more than that the days had come when it was night in the afternoon, and that he was given fewer political assignments. This was annoying, because Beasley's candidacy for the governorship had given me a personal interest in the political situation. Dowden explained:

DOWDEN. "Things are looking Dave's way. He's always worked hard for the party; not on the stump, of course; but the boys understand there are more important things than speech-making. His record in Congress gives him the confidence of everybody in the state, and, besides that, people always trust a quiet man. I tell you if nothing happens he'll get it."

BOOTH. Mr. Meyers at the Five and Dime had a ready opinion.

MR. MEYERS. "I'm FER Beasley, because he's Dave Beasley! Yes, sir, I'm FER him. You know the boys say if a man is only FOR you, in this state, there isn't much in it and he may go back on it; but if he's FER you, he means it. Well, I'm FER Beasley!"

BOOTH. There were other candidates, of course; none of them formidable; but I was surprised to learn of the existence of a small but energetic faction opposing our friend right here in Wainwright, his own town.

DOWDEN. "What are you surprised about? If St. Paul himself lived in Wainwright, he couldn't run for alderman without some folks trying to block him."

BOOTH. The head and front (and backbone, too) of the opposition to Beasley was a close-fisted, hard-knuckled, risen-from-the-soil sort of man, one named Simeon Peck. He possessed no inconsiderable influence, I heard; was a hard worker, and vigorously seconded by an energetic lieutenant, a young man named Grist. They were bitterly and eagerly opposed to Beasley's nomination, and worked without ceasing to prevent it. Dowden again provided clarity:

DOWDEN. "Grist's against us because he had a quarrel with a clerk in Beasley's office, and wanted Beasley to discharge him, and Beasley wouldn't; Sim Peck's against us out of just plain wrong-headedness, and because he never was for ANYTHING nor FER anybody in his life. I had a talk with the old mutton-head the other day; he said our candidate ought to be a farmer, a man of the common people, and when I asked him where he'd find anybody more a 'man of the common people' than Beasley, he said Beasley was 'too much of a society man' to suit him! The idea of Dave as a 'society man' was too much for me, and I laughed in Sim Peck's face, but that didn't stop Sim Peck!

PECK. Jest look at the style he lives in! Ain't he fairly LAPPED in luxury? Look at that big house he lives in! Look at the way he goes around in that carriage of his – and a colored servant to drive him half the time!'

DOWDEN. I had to laugh again, and, of course, that made Sim twice as mad as he started out to be; and he went off swearing he'd show ME. The only trouble he and Grist and that crowd could give us would be by finding out something against Dave, and they can't do that because there isn't anything to find out."

BOOTH. I shared his confidence on this latter score, but was somewhat less sanguine on some others. There were only two newspapers of any political influence in Wainwright, the "Despatch" and the "Journal," and neither had "come out" for him. Our rivals at the "Journal" especially, I knew, had some inclination to coquette with Peck, Grist, and Company. Altogether, their faction was not entirely to be ignored.

Thus, my thoughts were a great deal more occupied with Beasley's chances than with the holiday spirit that now breathed good cheer over the town. So little, indeed, had this spirit touched me that, I was surprised one evening when my editor said

EDITOR. "I'll be glad when to-morrow is over."

BOOTH. "What's the particular trouble with to-morrow?"

EDITOR. "Christmas. Always so tedious. Like Sunday." *(phone rings)* "Despatch."

BOOTH. "Christmas, to-morrow!"

It was Christmas Eve, and I hadn't known it! I paused in sudden loneliness, with pictures coming before me of long-ago Christmas Eves at home! – old Christmas Eves when there was a Tree –

EDITOR. "Snap out of it! One last thing to get done. Head on over to Sim Peck's, on Madison Street. He thinks he's got something on David Beasley, but won't say any more over the telephone. See what there is in it."

BOOTH. I left the office at a speed which must have given my superior the highest conception of my journalistic zeal. At a telephone station on the next corner I called up Mrs. Apperthwaite's house and asked for Dowden.

BOOTH. "What are you doing?"

DOWDEN. "Playing bridge."

BOOTH. "Are you going out anywhere?"

DOWDEN. "No. What's the trouble?"

BOOTH. "I'll tell you later. I may want to see you before I go back to the office."

DOWDEN. "All right. I'll be here all evening."

BOOTH. Down-town the streets were crowded with the package-laden people, bending heads and shoulders to the bitter wind. At corners it struck such a blow upon the chest of the pedestrians that for a moment it would halt them, and you could hear them gasping half-smothered "AHS" like bathers in a heavy surf. Yet there was a gayety in this eager gale; the crowds pressed anxiously, yet happily, up and down the street in their generous search for things to give away. It was not the rich who struggled through the cold to-night; these were people who carried their own bundles home. You saw them: toilers and savers, tired mothers and fathers, worn with the grinding thrift of all the year, but now for this one night careless of how hard-saved the money, reckless of everything but the joy of giving it to bring the children joy on the one great to-morrow. So they bent their heads to the freezing wind, their arms laden with daring bundles and their hearts uplifted with the tremulous happiness of giving more than they could afford. Meanwhile, Mr. Simeon Peck, honest man, had chosen this season to work harm if he might to the gentlest of his fellow-men.

PECK. "From the 'Despatch,' hay? That's good. We'd most give you up. This here's Mr. Grist,"

GRIST. "Mmh."

PECK. "Who feels the same way about Dave Beasley that I do. That other young feller, he's from the 'Journal.' Likely you're acquainted."

JOURNAL MAN. We haven't met. Bitter cold.

BOOTH. Indeed.

PECK. "I've got you newspaper men here, because I'm goin' to show you somep'n' about Dave Beasley that'll open a good many folk's eyes when it's in print."

BOOTH. "Well, what is it?"

PECK. "Jest hold your horses a little bit, Grist and me knows.

GRIST. "Heh."

PECK. "And I'm goin' to take you two reporters to LOOK at it and see for yourself. All ready? Then come on."

BOOTH. "Strange. What IS he up to?"

JOURNAL MAN. "I don't know any more than you do, he thinks he's got something that'll queer Beasley. Peck's an old fool, but it's just possible he's got hold of something. Nearly everybody has ONE thing, at least, that they don't want found out. It may be a good story. Lord, what a night!"

BOOTH. "Looks to snow before the night's out. See here, Mr. Peck – "

PECK. "You listen to ME, young man! I'm givin' you some news for your paper, and I'm gittin' at it my own way, but I'll git AT it, don't you worry! I'm goin' to let some folks around here know what kind of a feller Dave Beasley really is; yes, and I'm goin' to show George Dowden he can't laugh at ME!"

BOOTH. "You mean you're going to take Dowden on this expedition, too?"

PECK. "TAKE him! I guess HE'S at Beasley's, all right."

BOOTH. "No, he isn't; he's at Mrs. Apperthwaite's – playing cards."

PECK. "What!"

BOOTH. "I happen to know that he'll be there all evening."

PECK. "Grist!"

GRIST. "Eh?"

PECK. "Even Dowden ain't at Beasley's. Ain't the Lord workin' fer us to-night!"

GRIST. "Heh!"

BOOTH. "Why don't you take Dowden with you, if there's anything you want to show him?"

PECK. "By George, I WILL! Grist, I recken we'll pick up a recruit."

BOOTH. We headed into the cold and soon arrived at Mrs. Apperthwaite's.

PECK. "Grist."

GRIST. "Eh?"

PECK. "You and the journal man wait out here."

JOURNAL MAN. "Ok."

PECK. "You Despatch feller, you come with me."

BOOTH. "Alright."

PECK. "Jest step in and tell George Dowden that Sim Peck's out here and wants to see him at the door a minute. Be quick."

BOOTH. I went into the library, and there sat Dowden contemplatively playing bridge with Miss Apperthwaite. She quite took my breath away; she was dressed in honor of the Christmas Eve, and there was a sort of splendor about her. It detracted nothing from this that her expression was a little sad: something not uncommon with her lately. I had attributed it to Jean Valjean, though perhaps to-night it might have been due merely to bridge.

DOWDEN. "What is it?"

BOOTH. "Simeon Peck. He thinks he's got something on Beasley. He's waiting to see you."

DOWDEN. "Peck!"

BOOTH. "He's right outside."

PECK. "Oh, I'm here! I've come around to let you know that you couldn't laugh like a horse at ME no more, George Dowden! So YOU weren't invited, either."

DOWDEN. "Invited? Where?"

PECK. "Over to the BALL your friend is givin'."

DOWDEN. "What friend?"

PECK. "Dave Beasley. So you ain't quite good enough to dance with his high-society friends!"

DOWDEN. "What are you talking about?"

PECK. "I reckon you won't be quite so strong FER Beasley when you find he can use you in his BUSINESS, but when it comes to ENTERTAININ' – oh no, you ain't quite the boy!"

DOWDEN. "I'd appreciate your explaining!"

PECK. "Then I reckon you better come along. We be'n havin' kind of a consultation at my house over somep'n' Grist seen at Beasley's a little earlier in the evening."

BOOTH. "What did Grist see?"

PECK. "HACKS! Hacks drivin' up to Beasley's house – a whole lot of 'em. Grist was down the street a piece, and it was pretty dark, but he could see the lamps and hear the doors slam as the people got out. Besides, the whole place is lit up from cellar to attic. Grist come on to my house and told me about it, and I begun usin' the telephone; called up all the men that COUNT in the party – found most of 'em at home, too. I ast 'em if they was invited to this ball to-night; and not a one of 'em was. THEY'RE only in politics; they ain't high SOCIETY enough to be ast to Mr. Beasley's dancin'-parties! We're goin' to see what there is to see, and I'm goin' to have these boys from the newspapers write a full account of it. If you want to come along, I expect it'll do you a power o' good."

DOWDEN. "I'll go."

PECK. "Good. Grist!"

GRIST. "Mmh!"

PECK. "Got my recruit!"

GRIST. "Mmh!"

PECK. "I reckon he'll git a change of heart to-night!"

BOOTH. And now, sheltering my eyes from the stinging wind, I saw that Beasley's house WAS illuminated; every window, up stairs and down, was aglow with rosy light, although the shades were lowered.

PECK. "Look at that! Wha'd I tell you! How do you feel about it NOW?"

DOWDEN. "But where are the hacks?"

PECK. "Folks all come! Won't be no more hacks till they begin to go home. All right?"

JOURNAL MAN. "All right."

PECK. "Let's go git your story."

BOOTH. We had just started down the drive when something curious happened.

Beasley's front door was thrown open, and there stood Beasley himself. The bright hall behind him was beautiful with evergreen streamers and wreaths, and strain of dance-music wandered out to us as the door opened, but there was nobody except David Beasley in sight, which certainly seemed peculiar – for a ball!

BEASLEY. "Come right in, Colonel! I'd have sent a carriage for you if you hadn't telephoned me this afternoon that your rheumatism was so bad you didn't expect to be able to come. I'm glad you're well again. Yes, they're all here, and the ladies are getting up a quadrille in the sitting-room."

BOOTH. It was at this moment that I received upon the calf of the left leg a kick, the ecstatic violence of which led me to attribute it to Mr. Dowden.

BEASLEY. "Gentlemen's dressing-room up-stairs to the right, Colonel." *(door close)*

BOOTH. There was a pause of awed silence among us.

I improved it by returning the kick to Mr. Dowden.

JOURNAL MAN. "What in…?"

PECK. "By the Almighty! Who – WHAT was Dave Beasley talkin' to? There wasn't nobody THERE! He's crazy!"

JOURNAL MAN. "Get out! He saw us coming. He was giving us the laugh."

DOWDEN. "You think so?"

BOOTH. "I don't think so!"

JOURNAL MAN. "Aw, come on…"

PECK. "See here, boys, there's no use arguin'. One thing we're all agreed on: nobody here never seen no such a dam peculiar performance as WE jest seen in their whole lives before. THURfore, ball or NO ball, there's somep'n' mighty wrong about this business. Ain't that so, Grist?"

GRIST. "YEP!"

PECK. "Well, then, there's only one thing to do – let's find out what it is. Perhaps he ain't pulled all the shades down on the other side the house. Lots o' people fergit to do that."

BOOTH. He was right. Around the side we found an open window. Part of the room was clear to our view, though about half of it was shut off from us by the very king of all Christmas-trees, glittering with dozens and dozens of candles. Next to the Tree, his back against the wall, sat old Bob, seemingly alone. He was scraping a fiddle and the tune he played was, "Oh, my Liza, po' gal!" When he finished he said:

OLD BOB. "Now come de big speech."

BOOTH. The Honorable David Beasley stepped out from beyond the Christmas-tree. He bowed gracefully several times to the empty room.

PECK. "Well, don't this beat hell!"

JOURNAL MAN. "Look out! Ladies present."

BOOTH. "Where?"

JOURNAL MAN. "Just behind us. She followed us over from your boarding-house. She's been standing around near us all along."

BOOTH. I stepped to the cloaked figure I had been too absorbed in our quest to notice. It was Miss Apperthwaite.

MISS APPERTHWAITE. "I heard everything that man said in our hallway."

BOOTH. "So you couldn't HELP following!"

BEASLEY. "Ladies and gentlemen,"

MISS APPERTHWAITE. "Hush, he's saying something."

BEASLEY. "Ladies and gentlemen,"

BOOTH. "The only speech he's ever made in his life – and he's stuck!"

BEASLEY. "Ladies and gentlemen. Mr. and Mrs. Hunchberg, Colonel Hunchberg and AUNT COOLEY HUNCHBERG, Miss Molanna, Miss Queen, and Miss Marble Hunchberg, Mr. Noble, Mr. Tom, and Mr. Grandee Hunchberg, Mr. Corley Linbridge, and Master Hammersley: You see before you to-night, my person, merely the representative of your real host. MISTER Swift. Mister Swift has expressed a wish that there should be a speech, and has deputed me to make it. He requests that the subject he has assigned me should be treated in as dignified a manner as is possible – considering the orator. Ladies and gentlemen: I will now address you upon the following subject: 'Why we Call Christmas-time the Best Time.'

"Christmas-time is the best time because it is the kindest time. Nobody ever felt very happy without feeling very kind, and nobody ever felt very kind without feeling at least a LITTLE happy. So, of course, either way about, the happiest time is the kindest time – that's THIS time. The most beautiful things our eyes can see are the stars; and for that reason, and in remembrance of One star, we set candles on the tree to be stars in the house. So we make Christmas-time a time of stars indoors; and they shine warmly against the cold outdoors that is like the cold of other seasons not so kind. We set our hundred candles on the tree and keep them bright throughout the Christmas-time, for while they shine upon us we have light to see this life, not as a battle, but as the march of a mighty Fellowship! Ladies and gentlemen, I thank you!"

BOOTH. Old Bob again set his fiddle to his chin and scraped the preliminary measures of a quadrille.

BEASLEY. "TAKE your pardners! Balance ALL!

(**BEASLEY** *dances a quadrille with great enthusiasm, variously addressing his dancing partners.*)

Hooray!

BOOTH. I think the combination of abandon and decorum with which he performed that "Grand Right-and-Left" was the funniest thing I have ever seen.

PECK. "NOW do you believe me? Is he crazy, or ain't he?"

GRIST. "HMMphsrrrghr."

PECK. "Do you see where it puts US? We come out to buy a barn, and got a house and lot fer the same money. It's the greatest night's work I've ever done!"

GRIST. "Ehhh!"

(They shake.)

PECK. "This'll do the work! It's about two-thousand per cent better than the story we started to git. Why, Dave Beasley'll be in a padded cell in a month! It'll be all over town to-morrow, and he'll have as much chance fer governor as that fiddler in there! What do you think of your candidate NOW?"

DOWDEN. "Who came in the hacks that Grist saw?"

PECK. "Why – who in Halifax DID come in them hacks?"

BOOTH. "My money's on the Hunchbergs."

BEASLEY. Bravo! Bravo, bravo! YOU WERE A WONDER-FUL CORNER AUNT COOLEY! I beg your pardon, Miss Molanna, I'm afraid I stepped on your train. – And now, if the ladies will be so kind as to take the gentlemen's arms, we will proceed to the dining-room and partake of a slight collation."

BOOTH. Then into the vision of our paralyzed and dumfounded watchers came the little wagon, pulled by Old Bob, and there sat Hamilton Swift, Junior, his soul shining rapture out of his great eyes, a bright spot of color on each of his thin cheeks.

HAMILTON. "Oh, Cousin David Beasley, that was the BEAUTIFULLEST quadrille ever danced in the world! And, please, won't YOU take Mrs. Hunchberg out to supper?"

BEASLEY. *(bowing)* "Mrs. Hunchberg, may I have the honor?"

HAMILTON. "And I must have MISTER Hunchberg! He must walk with me."

BEASLEY. "He tells ME, he'll be mighty glad to. And there's a plate of bones for Simpledoria."

HAMILTON. "You lead the way, you and Mrs. Hunchberg."

BEASLEY. "Are we all in line? Now, let us on. Ho there! HOO-ray!"

HAMILTON. BR-R-RA-vo! Yes, Mr. Hunchberg, I agree. It's a wonderful party!

BOOTH. When they reached the door, old Bob rose, turned in after them, and, still fiddling, played the procession and himself down the hall.

And so they marched away, and we were left staring into the empty room…

JOURNAL MAN. "My soul! And he did all THAT – just to please a little sick kid!"

PECK. "I can't figure it out."

JOURNAL MAN. "I can! This story WILL be all over town to-morrow. It'll be all over town, though not in any of the papers – and I don't believe it's going to hurt Dave Beasley's chances any. Thank you for sending for me, You've given me a treat. I'm FER Beasley!"

BOOTH. Well Mr. Peck? You got anything else you want to say? Or you, Mr. Grist?

GRIST. No.

(**PECK & GRIST** *exit.*)

BOOTH. I thought not.

DOWDEN. "Well, sir, they were right about one thing: it certainly was mighty low down of Dave not to invite ME – and you, too – to his Christmas party. Let him go to thunder with his old invitations, I'm going in, anyway! Come on. I'm plum froze."

BOOTH. We trooped around to the front door and rang, loud and long. It was Beasley himself who opened it.

BEASLEY. "What in the name – ? What on earth are you fellows doing out here?"

BOOTH. "We've come to your Christmas party, you old high-stepper!"

BEASLEY. "HOO-ray! Well come on in, it's mighty cold out here!"

BOOTH. I waited a moment longer, and then it happened.

MISS APPERTHWAITE. "David, you've got so many lovely people in your house to-night: isn't there room for – for just one fool? It's Christmas-time!"

(They enter the house together. **BOOTH** *looks at us. He follows them inside.)*

End of Play

See what people are saying about
BEASLEY'S CHRISTMAS PARTY...

"A tiny seasonal treat (that) builds to an irresistibly charming climax...that good and bad always stay true, with good usually coming out ahead."
– Michael Feingold, *The Village Voice*

"In the holiday chests of many households, nestled in jumbles of ornaments and lights, there is one special heirloom, to be given pride of place on the Christmas tree: an old painted angel, perhaps, with history in its chipped wooden wings, or a faded star that outshines any flashy electric bulb. "*Beasley's Christmas Party* is a bit like such small treasures. Adapted from a 1909 story by Booth Tarkington, this heartfelt fable is a sweet, humble gift to the season.

"It's the thoughtfulness that counts. Keen Company's Carl Forsman doesn't try to gussy up the story or disguise its literary origins. The tale begins as something of a mystery story, but evolves—at a leisurely, fireside pace—into a touching exploration of imagination, loneliness and the virtue of kindness. In terms of dazzle, *Beasley's Christmas Party* can hardly compete with White Christmas or the Rockette launch at Radio City. It gets its Christmas cheer the old-fashioned way: It earns it."
– Adam Feldman, *Time Out New York*

www.ingramcontent.com/pod-product-compliance
Lightning Source LLC
Chambersburg PA
CBHW070420120726
47909CB00005B/1722